Usborne Vintage Fashion Coloring Book

Illustrated and designed
by Antonia Miller

Written by Ruth Brocklehurst

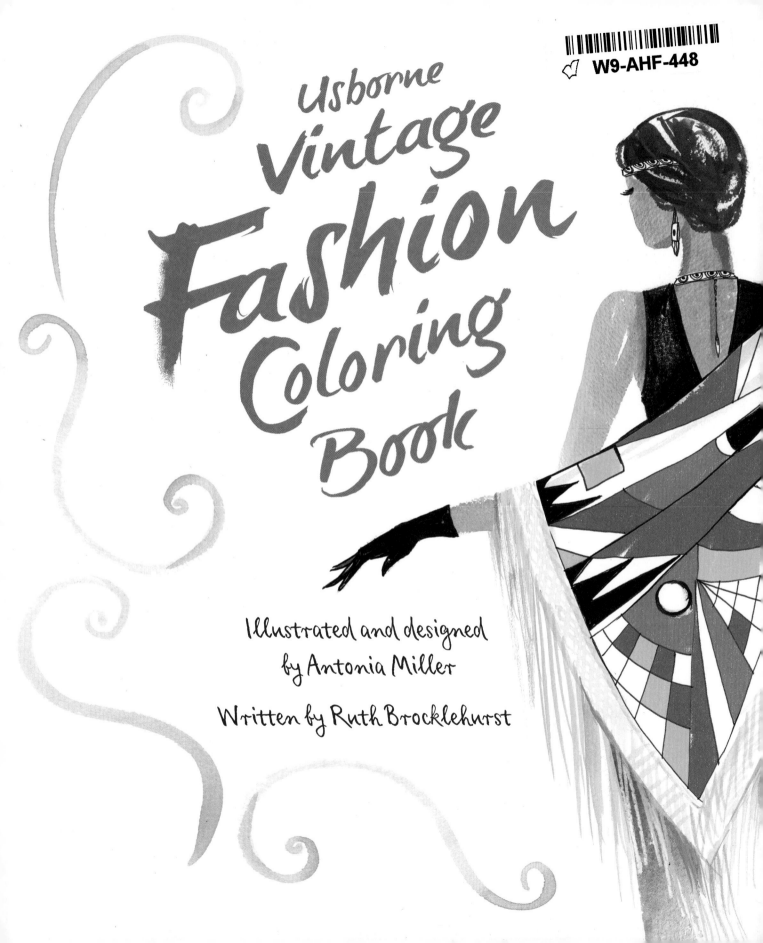

Style revival

Fashion changes every season. But now there's a new trend for vintage clothing – anything between 25 and 100 years old. This timeline shows some of the key looks through the decades.

1910s
First World War (1914-18)

Sailor collar

Straight, ankle-length dress

Practical clothes for wartime

1920s

Beaded decoration

Dropped waist

Pastel shades were often put with black.

Shorter, boxy dress shapes

1930s

Floppy hat

Sleeveless blouse

'Palazzo' pants

Red, white and blue were very popular.

Long, lean silhouettes

1940s
Second World War (1939-45)

Wide shoulders

Knee-length skirt

Tailored clothing

Styles limited by wartime fabric shortages

Nautical fashions based on sailors' clothing, with naval motifs in red, white and blue, have come around again and again in the last 100 years.

Pretty dresses in floral fabrics, usually in fresh pastel shades, have been in vogue for spring and summer in every decade.

Bright fabrics printed with so-called 'psychedelic' swirls and spiral patterns were popular in the 1960s and 70s, often in citrus shades, bright pinks and purples.

1950s

Rounded shoulders

Cinched-in waist

Fresh pastels or strong, bright shades

Full skirt

Feminine 'hourglass' silhouettes

1960s

This trend used zingy blocks of color.

Geometric print mini dress

Short dresses influenced by shapes of the 1920s

1970s

Mustard yellow, orange and brown

A-line maxi skirt

Loose, flowing clothes and bold prints

1980s

Cropped T-shirt

Harem pants

Anything goes – from sportswear to suits

In the 1920s and 1960s, fashion designers were inspired by modern art to use fabrics with bold geometric patterns.

Ball gowns

Late 1960s-70s

One-shoulder gown

Feather trim

1930s
Fishtail hemline with contrast stitching

1950s Floor-length gown

Satin evening gloves

Full skirt with net petticoats underneath for extra volume

Tiaras and jewels

1920s Drop earrings

1930s Hair jewel

1970s Silver and turquoise necklace and earrings

1930s Art Deco tiara

1930s Earrings and bracelet set

1950s Cocktail rings with bright gemstones

1920s Headband with beads and sequins

1930s Silver bracelets with semi-precious stones

1920s
Tiara with jewels and diamanté stars

1920s
Feathered flapper headband

1910s
Wreath-style tiara

1980s
Earrings

1950s
Earrings

1930s Hair jewel

1960s
Earrings made with plastic beads

1920s
Long string of beads

❧ Geometric prints ❧

1920s
Dress fabric with black and pastel geometric blocks

1920s
Bell-shaped cloche hat (cloche is French for 'bell')

Straight shift dress

Shawl with pattern influenced by Art Deco — a decorative style popular in the 1920s and 30s

1960s

A-line mini dress with hemline well above the knees

Bobbed hair

Cropped, boxy jacket

Knee-high boots

Black, white and primary color blocks

Bright striped tights

Ankle boots

Box bag with Art Deco design

Shirts and tops

1930s
Peasant blouse
with gathered neck

1970s
Long, pointed
shirt collar

1920s
Blouses with rounded
'Peter Pan' collars

Bright embroidered flowers

Cape collar

1930s
Balloon
sleeves

1940s
Puffed sleeves

1930s Frilled v-neck

1940s Keyhole neckline

'Peplum' skirt

1960s Secretary blouse with bow collar

1980s High-necked ruffle shirt

1980s Sweetheart neckline

Psychedelic swirls

Late 1960s
Circle dress
with bib front

Bright bubblegum shades

1960s
A-line
mini dress

Scarf with psychedelic print

1970s
Maxi dress
with flared
sleeves

Bright pink, purple and citrus swirls

Nautical fashion

1910s

1920s
Sailor collar

Red, white and blue plaid skirt

Striped plimsolls

1970s
Sundress with yacht print and narrow shoulder straps

Striped French fisherman's top – made fashionable by Coco Chanel

1950s
Sailor collar with a large contrasting bow

1930s
Wide 'palazzo' pants

Polka dot print skirt

Shoes and boots

1920s Dancing shoes

1940s Wedge-heeled sandal

1950s Striped stilettos

1930s Heeled shoe

1930s Two-tone brogue

1970s Slingback

1950s
Polka dot
peep-toe shoe

1920s Embroidered court shoe

1960s
Pumps with low,
square heels

1950s
Basketball boots first worn for fashion, as well as sports

1910s
Button-up boot

1970s
Platform sole with diamond pattern

1970s Clog

1980s Floral stiletto

1930s Canvas plimsolls

1970s Rainbow-striped loafer

~ Pants ~

1940s
Cuffed shorts

1930s
High-waisted 'palazzo' pants

1970s
Denim shorts with rainbows on the back pockets

1910s-30s
Jodhpurs worn for outdoor activities

Buttons at the cuffs

1970s
Bell-bottomed flares in bright floral print

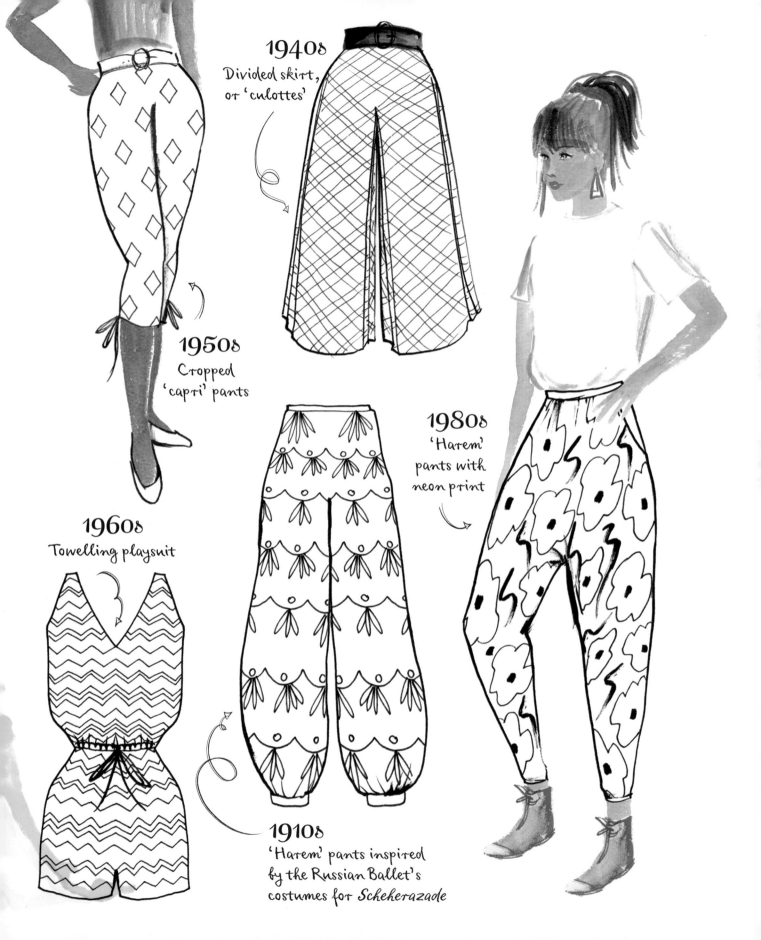

1940s
Divided skirt, or 'culottes'

1950s
Cropped 'capri' pants

1980s
'Harem' pants with neon print

1960s
Towelling playsuit

1910s
'Harem' pants inspired by the Russian Ballet's costumes for *Scheherazade*

Evening dresses

Early 1920s
Beaded decorations add sparkle

Late 1920s
Longer 'handkerchief' hem adds movement when dancing

1950s
Cocktail dress with full skirt

1950s
Evening dress with strapless bodice and asymmetric hem

1920s
Backless dress with ruffles

Attention drawn to the back

Shawl and gloves to match

Bags and purses

1980s Contrast bow

1960s

1920s Beaded purse

1930s Geometric design

Wooden handles

1970s

1960s Psychedelic print

1950s Basket bag with bright flower

1980s Color block shoulder bag

1930s Clutch purse

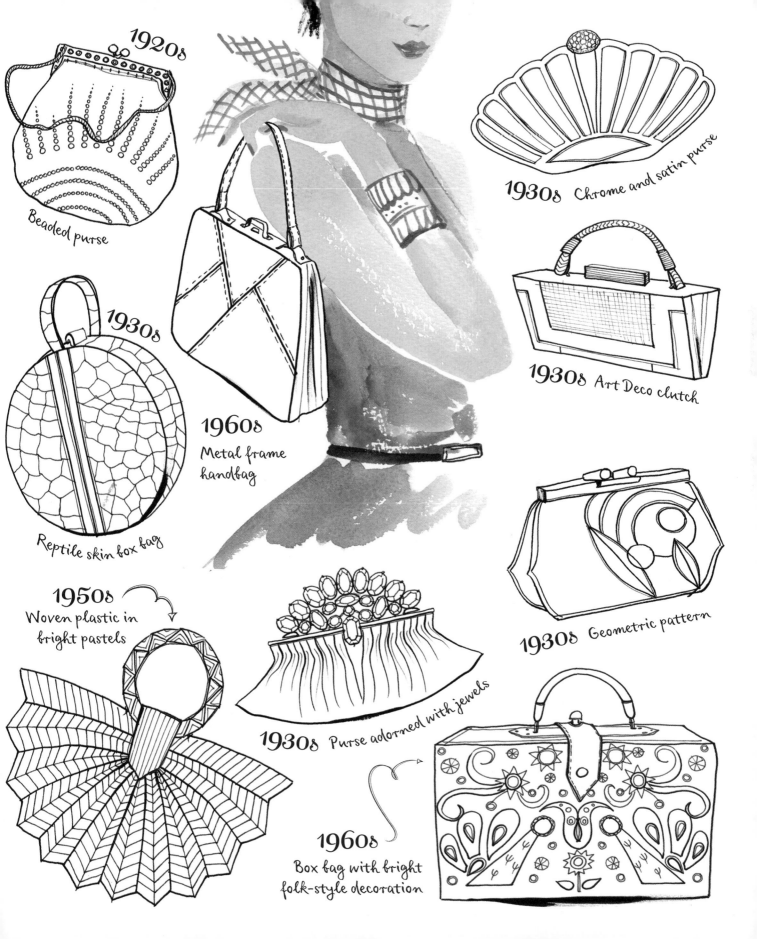

1920s

Beaded purse

1930s   Chrome and satin purse

1960s
Metal frame
handbag

1930s

1930s Art Deco clutch

Reptile skin box bag

1950s
Woven plastic in
bright pastels

1930s Geometric pattern

1930s Purse adorned with jewels

1960s
Box bag with bright
folk-style decoration

Floral dresses

Late 1920s
Floral fabric with contrasting bows

1980s
Tea dress with v-shaped 'cuirass' bodice

Asymmetric hemline just below the knee

Romantic roses inspired by Victorian fabrics

1950s
Cinched-in waist and full skirt

Hat worn slightly at an angle

1940s
Square shoulders with puffed sleeves

1930s
Small, stylized flowers

Large floral print combined with stripes

Gently flared skirt

Winter coats

Late 1940s
Tailored coat
with full skirt

Fur trim

1950s
Double-
breasted
cape

1920s
Kimono-style
wrap coat

Early 1960s
Cocoon coat in
pastel shades

1950s
Swing jacket with
funnel neck

Rich reds or jewel tones with dark fur trim

Hats and gloves

1930s Wide-brimmed straw hat

1950s Cone hat with large ribbon

1930s Zig zag pattern

1930s Satin evening glove

1980s Canvas bucket hat with band

1970s Floppy felt hat

1920s Embroidered evening gloves

1960s Striped glove

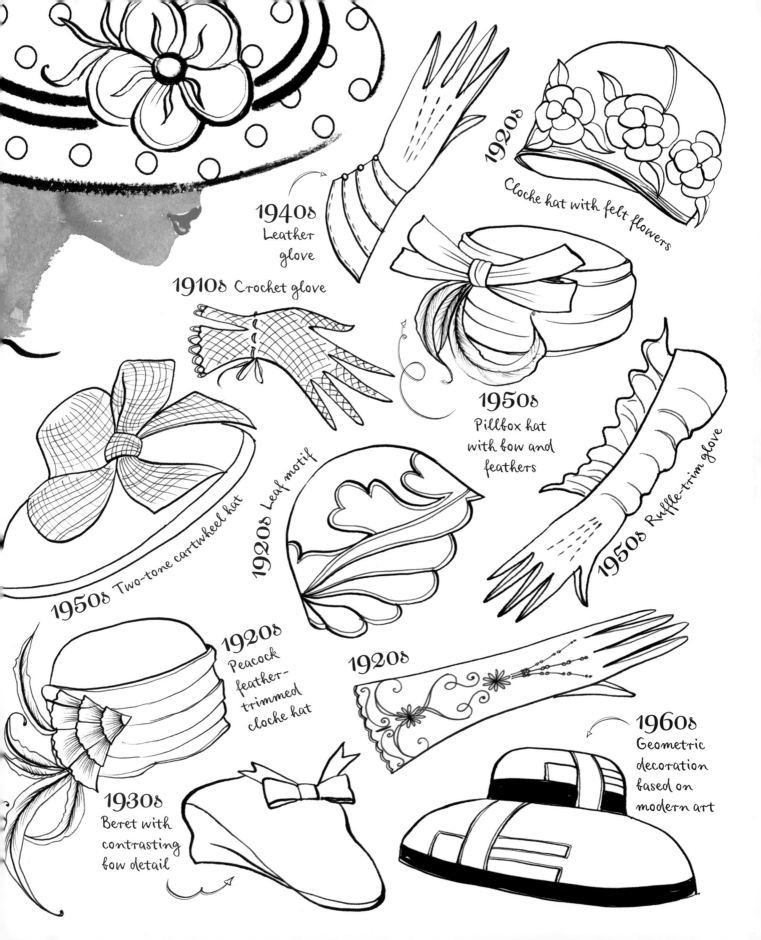

1940s Leather glove

1920s Cloche hat with felt flowers

1910s Crochet glove

1950s Pillbox hat with bow and feathers

1950s Two-tone cartwheel hat

1920s Leaf motif

1950s Ruffle-trim glove

1920s Peacock feather-trimmed cloche hat

1920s

1960s Geometric decoration based on modern art

1930s Beret with contrasting bow detail

Skirts

1940s
Fishtail skirt

1950s
Puffball or bubble skirt

1980s
Ra-ra skirt

1960s Mini kilt

Two-tone saddle shoes

1950s
Circle skirt with appliqué poodle motif

1960s
Dogtooth plaid
pencil skirt

1950s
Dirndl skirt

1970s
Maxi skirt

1950s
Tulip-shaped
skirt

Rainbow-striped A-line skirt

1970s

Brooches

1930s
Art Deco diamanté fan

1940s
Bluebird

1930s

1950s

1950s

1960s

1970s
Enamel owl

1940s
Felt anemone
flower corsage

1980s

1970s

1930s

❧ Usborne Quicklinks ❧

For links to websites where you can find out more about vintage fashion, go to the Usborne Quicklinks
Website at www.usborne.com/quicklinks and type in the title of this book. Please read our internet safety guidelines
on the Usborne Quicklinks Website. We recommend that children are supervised while using the internet.

First published in 2014 by Usborne Publishing Ltd., 83-85 Saffron Hill, London EC1N 8RT, England. www.usborne.com Copyright © 2014 Usborne Publishing Limited.